Zora's Zucchini

by KATHERINE PRYOR • illustrated by ANNA RAFF

Readers
to Eaters

San Francisco, California

For Celia & Michele. Little sisters make everything better. —K.P.

For the Committee. —A.R.

Text copyright © 2015 by Katherine Pryor
Illustrations copyright © 2015 by Anna Raff

Readers
to **Eaters**

READERS to EATERS
1620 Broadway, Suite 6, San Francisco, CA 94109
Distributed by Publishers Group West

ReadersToEaters.com

Printed in the U.S.A. by Worzalla, Stevens Point, WI

FSC
www.fsc.org
MIX
Paper from
responsible sources
FSC® C002589

Book design by Anna Raff
Book production by The Kids at Our House
The text is set in Billy.
The illustrations were made from ink and watercolor, colored digitally.
(hc) 10 9 8 7 6 5 4 3 2 1
(pb) 10 9 8 7 6 5 4 3
First Edition

Library of Congress Control Number: 2015937173
ISBN: 978-09836615-7-3 (hc)
ISBN: 978-09984366-1-6 (pb)

It was only the third day of summer vacation,
but Zora was already out of ideas.

Zora rode her bike in large, lazy circles around the neighborhood, just like the day before, and the day before that.

When Zora rode by the hardware store, she noticed something new—a bunch of plants with fuzzy green leaves.

"Free zoo-kee-nee," Zora read. "Z, like me."

She filled her basket with zucchini plants and headed home.

"Look what I found!" Zora announced. "Zucchini! I'm going to plant these in our garden."

Zora dug big holes so the roots had room to grow.

She settled the plants snugly in the soil.

She watered each one.

"That's going to be a *lot* of zucchini," said her father.

"We'll eat it!" Zora promised.

As June warm turned to July hot, Zora tended her garden. She watered the plants when their leaves got droopy. She cheered every time she saw a new yellow-orange zucchini blossom.

One morning, Zora spotted her very first zucchini!

She snapped it off the vine with a quick twist, and raced to show her family.

Zora's family found a new way to cook zucchini every day.
Her brother made bread. Her sister made soup. Her parents marinated
and grated and barbecued. As Zora's garden grew, they ate zucchini
for breakfast, lunch, and dinner.

"More?" Zora offered.

By the first day of August, Zora's garden was a jungle of prickly, tickly, bushy, blossomy plants. Every single one of those plants was covered in zucchini. There was no way her family could eat it all.

Zora peered into her neighbor's garden.
It was full of tomatoes, but no zucchini.

"Hi, Mrs. Thompson! Would you like to trade
some tomatoes for some zucchini?" Zora asked.

"Absolutely!" Mrs. Thompson replied.

Zora swapped an armful of zucchini for an armful of tomatoes.

Zora's zucchini kept growing.

"This is crazy!" she said.

She loaded up her bike and gave every last one away.

The next day, Zora found even *more* zucchini.
"Seriously?" she said.

Zora thought and thought. She had an idea,
but she knew she couldn't do it alone.

Her brother painted the signs.

Her parents printed the flyers.

Zora and her sister posted them all over the neighborhood.

On Saturday, Zora's Garden Swap was open for business.

TAKE A VEGGIE LEAVE A VEGGIE

or at least please take some zucchini

Zora straightened her sign. She checked the time. The sun got hotter, Zora's feet got fidgetier, and she began to worry that her Garden Swap was a Garden Flop.

or at least please

Then, Zora saw Mrs. Rivera carrying a big bowl of raspberries, and Mr. Peterson bringing potatoes. Neighbors stopped by with carrots, peppers, and green beans from their gardens. They shared plums, apricots, and cherries from their trees.

People left whatever they had too much of, and took whatever they wanted. Zora traded and traded until all her zucchini was gone.

Zora looked around at the busy, noisy jumble of munching, laughing, chatting neighbors. Her zucchini garden had brought so many people together!

She was already plotting what to grow next summer.

When Gardens Grow. . . and Grow. . . and Grow

Gardens are tricky. Some weeks, we see every last cherry tomato, lettuce leaf, and green bean as a miracle—almost too precious and perfect to eat. As the season progresses, and our gardens produce more food than we can possibly eat, we ask ourselves, "What was I thinking when I planted all of this?"

About one-third of the world's food is wasted, which means that all the water, work, and time it took to grow that food is also wasted. So, what can you do if you have extra food?

DONATE IT Consider donating your extra fruit and vegetables to a food bank in your town. Food banks are places people go when they don't have enough to eat, and fresh produce is often one of the hardest things for food banks to acquire and store. Many towns have fruit tree "gleaning" programs, where volunteers harvest fruit from their neighbors' trees and take it to a food bank or community kitchen.

PRESERVE IT Canning, pickling, freezing, and drying fruits and vegetables are all good ways to stretch the abundance of summer into the fall and winter months. Freezing or canning the zucchini you're tired of in August can help stock your freezer and cupboards full of delicious food for the year to come.

SHARE IT Host a harvest party for your school or neighborhood. Create a scavenger hunt in the garden, set up a garden swap, or exchange your favorite recipes. Sharing food with others is a great way to meet your neighbors, make new friends, and give back to your community, just like Zora.